DOVER
CHILDREN'S THRIFT CLASSICS

The Adventures of Pinocchio

CARLO COLLODI

Adapted by Bob Blaisdell
Illustrated by Thea Kliros

DOVER PUBLICATIONS, INC.
New York

DOVER CHILDREN'S THRIFT CLASSICS
EDITOR OF THIS VOLUME: CANDACE WARD

Bibliographical Note

This Dover edition, first published in 1995, is a new abridgment, by Bob Blaisdell, of a standard English translation of *Le Avventure di Pinocchio: Storia di un burattino* (1883) by Carlo Collodi. The illustrations and the introductory Note have been specially prepared for this edition.

Library of Congress Cataloging-in-Publication Data

Collodi, Carlo, 1826–1890.
    [Avventure di Pinocchio. English]
    The adventures of Pinocchio / Carlo Collodi ; adapted by Bob Blaisdell ; illustrated by Thea Kliros.
       p.   cm. — (Dover children's thrift classics)
    Summary: Pinocchio, a wooden puppet full of tricks and mischief, with a talent for getting into trouble, wants more than anything else to become a real boy.
    ISBN 0-486-28840-4 (pbk.)
    [1. Puppets—Fiction. 2. Fairy tales.] I. Blaisdell, Robert. II. Kliros, Thea, ill. III. Title. IV. Series.
PZ8.C7Ad   1995
[Fic]—dc20   95–23471
                                            CIP
                                            AC

Manufactured in the United States of America
Dover Publications, Inc., 31 East 2nd Street, Mineola, N.Y. 11501

Note

Writing under the pen name Carlo Collodi, Carlo Lorenzini (1826–1890) was a journalist turned children's author. Among his works for young people were an Italian translation of Perrault's tales (c. 1875) and a series of amusing instructional books, the first of which was titled *Giannettino* (1876). But Lorenzini's most famous work was the history of the mischievous boy-puppet Pinocchio.

Lorenzini first introduced Pinocchio in an Italian children's magazine, the *Giornale dei bambini*, on July 7, 1881. The serial was published in book form in 1883 and enjoyed immediate success, as did its English translation when it was published in 1892.

The edition presented here relates Pinocchio's most exciting and memorable adventures. With the help of a talking Cricket and a good Fairy, Pinocchio learns some of the more difficult lessons of childhood and eventually realizes his dream of becoming a real live boy.

Contents

I

Pinocchio's First Pranks

ONCE UPON A TIME, there was a piece of wood. It was just a common block of firewood, one of those thick, solid logs that are put on the fire in winter to make cold rooms cozy and warm.

One day this piece of wood found itself in the shop of an old carpenter named Mastro Antonio. As soon as he saw that piece of wood, Antonio was filled with joy. "This has come in the nick of time. I shall use it to make the leg of a table."

He grasped the hatchet to peel off the bark and shape the wood.

But as he was about to give it the first blow, he heard a wee, little voice say: "Please be careful! Do not hit me so hard!"

1

Antonio turned his frightened eyes about the room
to find out where that wee, little voice had come from
and he saw no one! He returned to his work and
struck a solid blow upon the piece of wood.

"Oh, oh! You hurt!" cried the same faraway little
voice.

Antonio fell silent, his eyes popped out of his head,
his mouth opened wide, and his tongue hung down
on his chin. As soon as he regained the use of his
senses, he said, "Where did that voice come from?
Might it be that this piece of wood has learned to
weep and cry like a child?" He listened for the tiny
voice to moan and cry. He waited two minutes—
nothing; five minutes—nothing; ten minutes—
nothing.

The poor fellow was scared half to death, so he tried to sing a merry song in order to gain courage.

He set aside the hatchet and picked up the plane to make the wood smooth and even, but as he drew it to and fro, he heard the same tiny voice. This time it giggled as it spoke: "Stop it! Oh, stop it! Ha, ha, ha! You tickle my stomach."

At that very instant, a loud knock sounded on the door. "Come in," said the carpenter.

The door opened and a dapper little old man came in. His name was Geppetto, and he wore a wig the color of yellow corn.

"Good day, Mastro Antonio," said Geppetto.

"What brought you here, friend Geppetto?"

"My legs. This morning a fine idea came to me. I thought of making myself a beautiful wooden puppet. It must be wonderful, one that will be able to dance, fight with a sword and turn somersaults. With it I intend to go around the world. Will you give me a piece of wood to make this puppet?"

Mastro Antonio went to his bench to get the piece of wood which had frightened him so much. He gave it to Geppetto, who thanked him, and went away toward home.

Little as Geppetto's house was, it was neat and comfortable. It was a small room on the ground floor, with a tiny window under the stairway. The furniture could not have been much simpler: an old chair, an old bed and a table. As soon as he reached home, Geppetto took his tools and began to cut and shape the wood into a puppet.

He said to himself. "I think I'll call him Pinocchio," and set to work to make the hair, the forehead, the eyes. Imagine his surprise when he noticed that these eyes moved and then stared at him. Geppetto, seeing this, felt insulted, and said: "Ugly wooden eyes, why do you stare so?"

There was no answer.

After the eyes, Geppetto made the nose, which began to stretch as soon as finished. It stretched and stretched and stretched till it became so long, it seemed endless.

Poor Geppetto kept cutting it and cutting it, but the more he cut, the longer grew that rude nose. In despair he let it alone.

Next he made a mouth.

No sooner was it finished than it began to laugh and poke fun at him.

"Stop laughing!" said Geppetto.

The mouth stopped laughing, but it stuck out a long tongue.

Not wishing to start an argument, Geppetto made believe he saw nothing and went on with his work.

After the mouth, he made the chin, the shoulders, the stomach, the arms and the hands.

As he was about to put the last touches on the fingertips, Geppetto felt his wig being pulled off. He glanced up and what did he see? His yellow wig was in the puppet's hand.

"Pinocchio, give me my wig!"

But instead of giving it back, Pinocchio put it on his own head, which was half swallowed up in it.

"Pinocchio, you wicked boy!" Geppetto cried out. "You are not yet finished, and you start out by being rude to your poor old father. Very bad, my son, very bad!"

The legs and feet still had to be made. As soon as they were done, he took hold of the puppet under the arms and put him on the floor to teach him to walk.

Pinocchio's legs were so stiff that he could not move them, and Geppetto held his hand and showed him how to put out one foot after the other.

When his legs were loosened up, Pinocchio started walking by himself and ran all around the room. He came to the open door, and with one leap he was out into the street. Away he flew!

Poor Geppetto ran after him but was unable to catch him, for Pinocchio ran in leaps and bounds, his two wooden feet, as they beat on the stones of the street, making as much noise as twenty people in wooden shoes.

"Catch him! Catch him!" Geppetto kept shouting. But the people in the street, seeing a wooden puppet running like the wind, stood still to stare and to laugh.

By sheer luck, a policeman happened along, who, hearing all that noise, came and grabbed Pinocchio by the nose (it was an extremely long one and seemed made on purpose for that very thing) and returned him to Mastro Geppetto.

The little old man wanted to pull Pinocchio's ears. Think how he felt when, upon searching for them, he discovered that he had forgotten to make them!

All he could do was to seize Pinocchio by the back of the neck. As he was doing so, he shook him two or three times and said to him: "When we get home, then we'll settle this matter!"

Pinocchio, on hearing this, threw himself on the ground and refused to take another step. One person after another gathered around the two.

"Poor puppet," called out one man. "I am not surprised he doesn't want to go home. Geppetto, perhaps, will beat him!"

"Geppetto looks like a good man," added another, "but with boys he seems to be a real tyrant."

They said so much that, finally, the policeman ended matters by setting Pinocchio free and dragging Geppetto to prison.

What happened after this is almost unbelievable.

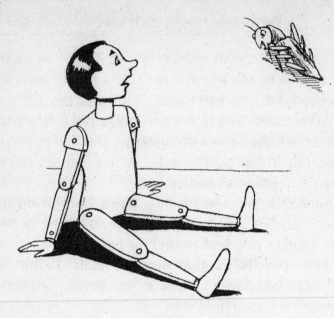

II

Pinocchio Promises to Go to School

ON REACHING HOME, Pinocchio slipped into the room, locked the door, and threw himself on the floor, happy at his escape.

But his happiness lasted only a short time, for just then he heard someone saying, "Cri-cri-cri!"

"Who is calling me?" asked Pinocchio, greatly frightened.

"I am!"

Pinocchio turned and saw a large cricket crawling slowly up the wall.

"Tell me, Cricket, who are you?"

"I am the Talking Cricket and I have been living in this room for one hundred years."

"Today, however, this room is mine," said the puppet, "and if you wish to do me a favor, get out now, and don't turn around even once."

"I refuse to leave this spot," answered the Cricket, "until I have told you a great truth."

"Tell it, then, and hurry."

"Woe to the boys who refuse to obey their parents and run away from home! They will never be happy in this world, and when they are older they will be very sorry for it."

"Sing on, Cricket, as you please. What I know is, that tomorrow, at dawn, I leave this place forever. If I stay here, the same thing will happen to me which happens to all other boys and girls. They are sent to school, and, whether they want to or not, they must study. As for me, let me tell you, I hate to study! It's much more fun, I think, to chase after butterflies, climb trees and steal birds' nests."

"Poor silly boy! Don't you know that if you go on like that, you will grow into a perfect donkey and that you'll be the laughingstock of everyone?"

"Keep still, you ugly Cricket!" cried Pinocchio.

But the Cricket continued: "If you do not like going to school, why don't you at least learn a trade, so that you can earn an honest living?"

"Shall I tell you something?" asked Pinocchio. "Of all the trades in the world, there is only one that really suits me."

"And what can that be?"

"That of eating, drinking, sleeping, playing and wandering around from morning till night."

"Let me tell you, for your own good, Pinocchio," said the Talking Cricket, "that those who follow that trade always end up in the hospital or in prison."

"Careful, ugly Cricket! If you make me angry you'll be sorry!"

"Poor Pinocchio, I am sorry for you."

"Why?"

"Because you are a puppet and, what is much worse, you have a wooden head."

At these words, Pinocchio jumped up, took a hammer from the bench and threw it with all his strength at the Talking Cricket. Perhaps he did not think he would strike it. But, sad to say, he did hit the Cricket, straight on its head.

With a last weak "cri-cri-cri" the poor Cricket fell from the wall, dead!

If the Cricket's death scared Pinocchio at all, it was only for a very few minutes. For, as night came on, a strange feeling at the pit of his stomach reminded the puppet that he had eaten nothing as yet.

He ran about the room, dug in all the boxes and drawers, and even looked under the bed in search of a piece of bread, hard though it might be, or a cookie, or perhaps a bit of fish. But he found nothing.

He wept and wailed to himself: "The Talking Cricket was right. It was wrong of me to disobey Father and to run away from home. If he were here now, I wouldn't be so hungry! Oh, how horrible it is to be hungry!"

And as his stomach kept grumbling more than ever and he had nothing to quiet it with, he thought of going out for a walk to the nearby village, in the hope of finding some charitable person who might give him a bit of bread.

In a dozen leaps and bounds, he came to the village, tired out, puffing like a whale, and with tongue hanging.

The whole village was dark and deserted. The stores were closed. In the streets, not even a dog could be seen. Pinocchio, in desperation, ran up to a doorway, threw himself upon the bell, and pulled it wildly, saying to himself: "Someone will surely answer that!"

He was right. An old man in a nightcap opened the window and looked out. He called down: "What do you want at this hour of night?"

"Will you be good enough to give me a bit of bread? I am hungry."

"Wait a minute, and I'll come right back," answered the old fellow, thinking he had to deal with one of those boys who love to roam around at night ringing people's bells while they are peacefully asleep.

After a minute or two, the same voice cried: "Get under the window and hold out your hat!"

Pinocchio had no hat, but he managed to get under the window just in time to feel a shower of ice-cold water pour down on his poor wooden head, his shoulders and over his whole body.

He returned home as wet as a rat, and tired out from hunger. He sat down on a little stool and put his two feet on the stove to dry them.

There he fell asleep, and while he slept, his wooden feet began to burn. Slowly, very slowly, they blackened and turned to ashes.

Pinocchio snored away happily, as if his feet were not his own. At dawn he opened his eyes just as a loud knocking sounded at the door.

"Who is it?" he called.

"It is I," answered Geppetto's voice.

The poor puppet, who was still half asleep, had not yet found out that his two feet were burned and gone. As soon as he heard his father's voice, he jumped up from his seat to open the door, but, as he did so, he staggered and fell headlong to the floor.

"Open the door for me!" Geppetto shouted.

"Father, dear Father, I can't," answered the puppet.

"Why can't you?"

"Because someone has eaten my feet."

"And who has eaten them?"

"The cat," answered Pinocchio, seeing that animal busily playing with some wood shavings in the corner of the room.

Geppetto, thinking this was only another prank of Pinocchio, climbed up the side of the house and went in through the window. At first he was very angry, but on seeing Pinocchio stretched out on the floor and really without feet, he felt very sad and sorrowful. Picking him up from the floor, he petted him, talking to him while the tears ran down his cheeks: "My little Pinocchio, my dear little Pinocchio! How did you burn your feet?"

"I don't know, Father, but believe me, the night has been a terrible one and I shall remember it as long as I live. I fell asleep and now my feet are gone but my hunger isn't!"

Geppetto felt sorry for him and, pulling three pears out of his pocket, offered them to him, saying: "These three pears were for my breakfast, but I give them to you gladly. Eat them and stop weeping."

"If you want me to eat them," said Pinocchio, "please peel them for me."

"Peel them?" asked Geppetto. "I should never have thought, dear boy of mine, that you were so dainty and fussy about your food. Bad, very bad! In this world, even as children, we must accustom ourselves

to eat of everything, for we never know what life may hold in store for us!"

"You may be right," answered Pinocchio, "but I will not eat the pears if they are not peeled. I don't like them."

And good old Geppetto took out a knife, peeled the three pears and put the skins in a row on the corner of the table.

Pinocchio ate one pear in a twinkling and started to throw the core away, but Geppetto held his arm.

"Oh, no, don't throw it away! Everything in this world may be of some use!"

"But the core I will not eat!" cried Pinocchio in an angry tone.

"Who knows?" repeated Geppetto calmly.

And later the three cores were placed on the table next to the skins. Pinocchio had eaten the three pears, and then he wailed, "I'm still hungry!"

"But I have no more to give you. I have only these cores and these skins."

"Very well, then," said Pinocchio, "if there is nothing else I'll eat them."

At first he made a face, but one after another, the skins and the cores disappeared.

The puppet, now that his hunger was gone, started to grumble and cry that he wanted a new pair of feet.

"Why should I make your feet over again? To see you run away from home once more?"

"I promise you," answered the puppet, "that from now on I'll be good."

"Boys always promise that when they want something," said Geppetto.

"I promise to go to school every day, to study, and to succeed—"

"Boys always sing that song when they want their own way."

"But I am not like other boys! I am better than all of them and I always tell the truth. I promise you, Father, that I'll learn a trade and I'll be the comfort and staff of your old age."

Geppetto, though trying to look very stern, felt his eyes fill with tears and his heart soften when he saw Pinocchio so unhappy. He said no more, but taking his tools and two pieces of wood, he set to work.

In less than an hour two strong, quick little feet were finished.

Geppetto said to the puppet: "Close your eyes and sleep!"

Pinocchio closed his eyes and pretended to be asleep, while Geppetto stuck on the two feet with a bit of glue.

As soon as the puppet felt his new feet, he gave one leap from the table and started to skip and jump around, as if he had lost his head from very joy.

"To show you how grateful I am to you, Father, I'll go to school now. But to go to school I need a suit of clothes."

Geppetto did not have a penny in his pocket, so he made his son a little suit of flowered paper, a pair of shoes from the bark of a tree and a tiny cap from a bit of dough.

Pinocchio ran to look at his reflection, and he felt so happy and proud. But then he said, "In order to go to school, I still need something very important—an ABC book."

"To be sure! But how shall we get it?"

"That's very easy. We'll go to a bookstore and buy it."

"And the money?"

"I have none."

"Neither have I," said the old man sadly. All at once, however, Geppetto jumped up from his chair. Putting on his old coat, full of darns and patches, he ran out of the house.

After a while he returned. In his hands he had the ABC book for his son, but the old coat was gone. The poor fellow was in his shirt sleeves and the day was cold.

"Where's your coat, Father?"

"I have sold it."

"Why did you sell your coat?"

"It was too warm."

Pinocchio understood the answer, and, unable to restrain his tears, he jumped on his father's neck and kissed him over and over.

III
At the Puppet Theater

A S THE PUPPET walked along to school with his new ABC book, his brain was busy planning hundreds of wonderful things. Talking to himself, he said, "In school today, I'll learn to read, tomorrow to write, and the day after tomorrow I'll do arithmetic. Then, clever as I am, I can earn a lot of money. With the very first pennies I make, I'll buy Father a new cloth coat. Cloth, did I say? No, it shall be of gold and silver with diamond buttons. That poor man certainly deserves it; for, after all, isn't he in his shirt sleeves because he was good enough to buy a book for me? On this cold day, too! Fathers are indeed good to their children!"

As he talked to himself, he thought he heard sounds of pipes and drums coming from a distance. He stopped to listen. Those sounds came from a little street that led to a small village along the shore. "What can that noise be? What a nuisance that I have to go to school! Otherwise . . ."

There he stopped, very much puzzled. He felt he had to make up his mind for either one thing or another. Should he go to school, or should he follow the pipes?

"Today I'll follow the pipes, and tomorrow I'll go to school. There's always plenty of time to go to school," decided the little rascal at last.

He started down the street, going like the wind. Suddenly, he found himself in a large square, full of people standing in front of a little wooden building painted in bright colors.

"What is that house?" Pinocchio asked a little boy near him.

"Read the sign and you'll know."

"I'd like to read, but somehow I can't today."

"Oh really? Then I'll read it to you: GREAT PUPPET THEATER."

"And how much does one pay to get in?"

Four pennies."

Pinocchio, who was wild with curiosity to know what was going on inside, said to the boy, "Will you give me four pennies until tomorrow?"

"I'd give them to you gladly," answered the boy, "but just now I can't give them to you."

"For the price of four pennies, I'll sell you my coat."

"If it rains, what shall I do with a coat of flowered paper?"

"Do you want to buy my shoes?"

"They are only good enough to light a fire with."

"What about my hat?"

"Fine bargain indeed! A cap of dough! The mice might come and eat it from my head!"

Pinocchio was almost in tears. At last he said, "Will you give me four pennies for the book?"

"I am a boy and I buy nothing from boys," said the little fellow.

"I'll give you four pennies for your ABC book," said a ragpicker who stood nearby.

Then and there, the book changed hands. And to think that poor old Geppetto sat at home shivering with cold, having sold his coat to buy that little book for his son!

Pinocchio disappeared into the Puppet Theater. The curtain was up and the performance had started. Harlequin and Pulcinella were reciting on the stage and, as usual, they were threatening each other with sticks and blows.

The play continued for a few minutes, and then suddenly, without any warning, Harlequin stopped talking. Turning toward the audience, he pointed to the rear of the theater, yelling wildly, "Look, look! Do I really see Pinocchio there?"

"Yes, yes! It is Pinocchio!" screamed Pulcinella.

"It is Pinocchio! It is Pinocchio!" yelled all the puppets, pouring out of the wings. "It is Pinocchio. It is our brother Pinocchio!"

"Pinocchio, come up to me," shouted Harlequin. "Come to the arms of your wooden brothers!"

Pinocchio leaped up on stage.

It was a heartbreaking sight, but the audience, seeing that the play had stopped, became angry and began to yell: "The play, the play, we want the play!"

The puppets, however, lifted Pinocchio on their shoulders and carried him around the stage in triumph!

At that moment the director came out of his room. He had such a fearful appearance that one look at him would fill you with horror. His beard was black, and so long that it reached from his chin down to his feet. His mouth was as wide as an oven, his teeth like yellow fangs, and his eyes, two glowing coals.

"Why have you brought such excitement into my theater?" the huge fellow asked Pinocchio.

"Believe me, your honor, the fault was not mine."

The director, whose name was Fire Eater, ordered Pinocchio brought to his kitchen by Harlequin and

Pulcinella. "He looks as if he were made of well-seasoned wood. He'll make a fine fire for my roast lamb."

Harlequin and Pulcinella hesitated a bit. Then, frightened by a look from Fire Eater, they obeyed him. They carried poor Pinocchio, who was wriggling and squirming like an eel and crying, "Father, save me! I don't want to die! I don't want to die!"

Fire Eater was very ugly, but far from being as bad as he looked. When he saw the poor puppet being brought in to him, struggling and crying, he felt sorry for him and gave a loud sneeze. While other people, when sad, weep and wipe their eyes, Fire Eater had the strange habit of sneezing.

Harlequin smiled and whispered to Pinocchio: "Good news, brother! Fire Eater has sneezed and this is a sign that he feels sorry for you. You are saved!"

Fire Eater said to Pinocchio: "Stop crying! Your wails give me a funny feeling!" Two loud sneezes finished his speech.

"God bless you!" said Pinocchio.

"Thanks! Are your father and mother still living?" asked Fire Eater.

"My father, yes. My mother I have never known."

"Your poor father would suffer terribly if I were to use you as firewood. However, I ought to be sorry for myself, too, just now. I have no more wood for the fire and the lamb is only half-cooked. Never mind! In your place I'll burn some other puppet. Hey there! Officers!"

At the call, two wooden officers appeared with funny hats on their heads and swords in their hands.

Fire Eater yelled, "Take Harlequin, tie him, and throw him on the fire. I want my lamb well done."

Think how poor Harlequin felt! He fell to the floor in fright.

Pinocchio, seeing this, threw himself at the feet of the Fire Eater and asked in a tearful voice, "Have pity, I beg of you."

"Well, what do you want from me now, puppet?"

"I beg for mercy for my poor friend Harlequin, who has never done the least harm in his life."

"There is no mercy here, Pinocchio. I have spared you. Harlequin must burn in your place. I am hungry and my dinner must be cooked."

"In that case," said Pinocchio, "my duty is clear. Come, officers! Tie me up and throw me on those flames. It is not fair for poor Harlequin, the best friend I have in the world, to die in my place."

These brave words made all the other puppets cry. Even the officers, who were made of wood also, cried like two babies.

Fire Eater at first remained hard and cold as a piece of ice; but then, little by little, he softened and began to sneeze. And after four or five sneezes, he opened wide his arms and said to Pinocchio: "You are a brave boy! I pardon Harlequin. Tonight I shall have to eat my lamb only half-cooked."

At the news that a pardon had been given, the puppets ran to the stage and danced and sang till dawn.

IV

The Fox and the Cat

THE NEXT DAY FIRE EATER called Pinocchio aside and asked him: "What is your father's name and what does he do?"

"Geppetto. He's a wood carver."

"Does he earn much?"

"He earns so much he never has a penny in his pockets. Just think that, in order to buy me an ABC book for school, he had to sell the only coat he owned."

"Poor fellow! I feel sorry for him. Here, take these five gold pieces. Go, give them to him with my kindest regards."

Pinocchio thanked him a thousand times. He then kissed the puppets goodbye and set out on his homeward journey.

He had gone barely half a mile when he met a lame Fox and a blind Cat, walking together like two good friends. The lame Fox leaned on the Cat, and the blind Cat let the Fox lead him along.

"Good morning, Pinocchio," said the Fox.

"How do you know my name?" asked the puppet.

"I saw your father yesterday standing at the door of his house. He was in his shirt sleeves trembling with cold."

25

"Poor father! But, after today, he will suffer no longer."

"Why?"

"Because I have become a rich man."

"You, a rich man?" said the Fox.

"Yes," said Pinocchio, "look at these five new gold pieces." And he pulled out the gold pieces Fire Eater had given him.

At the tinkle of gold, the Fox held out his paw that was supposed to be lame, and the Cat opened wide his two eyes, but he closed them again so that Pinocchio did not notice.

"I want to buy a new coat for my father," said Pinocchio. "After that, I'll buy an ABC book for myself."

"Do you want one hundred, a thousand, two thousand gold pieces for your miserable five?" asked the Fox.

"Yes, but how?"

"The way is very easy. Instead of returning home, come with us to the city of Simple Simons."

Pinocchio thought a while and then said firmly, "No, I don't want to go. Home is near, and I'm going where father is waiting for me. How unhappy he must be that I have not yet returned! I have been a bad son, and the Talking Cricket was right when he said that a disobedient boy cannot be happy in this world."

"Well, then," said the Fox, "if you really want to go home, go ahead, but you'll be sorry!"

"You'll be sorry," repeated the Cat.

"Think well, Pinocchio," said the Fox, "tomorrow your five gold pieces will be two thousand!"

"But how can they possibly become so many?"

"You must know," said the Fox, "that just outside the city of Simple Simons, there is a blessed field called the Field of Wonders. In this field you dig a hole and in the hole you bury a gold piece. After covering up the hole with earth, you water it well, sprinkle a bit of salt on it, and go to bed. During the night, the gold piece sprouts, grows, blossoms, and the next morning you find a beautiful tree, loaded with twenty-five hundred gold pieces."

"Fine, fine!" cried Pinocchio, dancing about with joy. "And as soon as I have them, I shall keep two thousand for myself and the other five hundred I'll give to you two."

"A gift for us?" cried the Fox. "Why, of course not!"

"Of course not!" repeated the Cat.

"We do not work for gain," said the Fox. "We work only to enrich others."

"To enrich others," repeated the Cat.

"What good people!" thought Pinocchio to himself. And forgetting his father, the new coat, the ABC book and all his good resolutions, he said to the Fox and to the Cat: "Let us go."

Cat and Fox and the puppet walked and walked and walked. At last, toward evening, dead tired, they came to the Inn of the Red Lobster. "Let us stop here awhile," said the Fox, "to eat a bite and rest for a few hours."

After eating, Pinocchio went to one room, and the Cat and Fox to another. As soon as the puppet was in bed, he fell fast asleep. When he woke up at midnight, the innkeeper told him that his friends had left two hours before.

"Where did my good friends say they would wait for me?" asked Pinocchio.

"At the Field of Wonders, at sunrise."

Pinocchio paid a gold piece for the three suppers and started on his way toward the field that was to make him a rich man.

He walked on, not knowing where he was going, for it was dark. Round about him not a leaf stirred. A few bats skimmed his nose now and again and scared him half to death. Once or twice he shouted: "Who goes there?" and the faraway hills echoed back to him: "Who goes there? Who goes . . .?"

As he walked, Pinocchio noticed a tiny insect glimmering on the trunk of a tree, a small being that glowed with a pale, soft light.

"Who are you?" he asked.

"I am the ghost of the Talking Cricket."

"What do you want?" asked the puppet.

"I want to give you a few words of good advice. Return home and give the four gold pieces you have left to your poor father who is weeping because he has not seen you for many a day."

"Tomorrow my father will be a rich man, for these four gold pieces will become thousands."

"Don't listen to those who promise you wealth overnight, my boy. As a rule they are either fools or swindlers! Listen to me and go home."

"But I want to go on!"

"Remember that boys who insist on having their own way sooner or later come to grief."

"The same nonsense! Goodbye, Cricket."

"Good night, Pinocchio, and may Heaven preserve you from the murderers!"

"We boys are really very unlucky," said the puppet to himself, as he once more set out on his journey into the darkness. "Everybody scolds us, everybody gives us advice, everybody warns us. If we were to allow it, everyone would try to be father and mother to us; everyone, even the Talking Cricket. Just because I would not listen to that bothersome Cricket, who knows how many troubles may be awaiting me! Murderers indeed!"

Pinocchio paused, however, for he thought he heard a slight rustle among the leaves behind him.

He turned to look, and behold, there in the darkness, stood two big black shadows, wrapped from head to foot in black sacks. The two figures leaped toward him as softly as if they were ghosts.

"Here they come!" Pinocchio said to himself, and, not knowing where to hide the gold pieces, he stuck all four of them under his tongue.

He tried to run away, but hardly had he taken a step, when he felt his arms grasped and heard two horrible, deep voices say to him:

"Your money or your life!"

On account of the gold pieces in his mouth, Pinocchio could not say a word, so he tried with head and hands and body to show, as best he could, that he was only a poor puppet without a penny in his pocket.

"Come, come, less nonsense, and out with your money!" cried one thief. "Out with your money or you're a dead man!"

"Dead man," repeated the other.

"And after having killed you," said the first, "we will kill your father also."

"No, no, not my father!" cried Pinocchio; but as he screamed, the gold pieces tinkled together in his mouth.

"Ah, you rascal, so that's the game! You have the money hidden under your tongue. Out with it!"

"Out with it!" repeated the other.

One of them grabbed the puppet by the nose and the other by the chin, and they pulled him from side to side to make him open his mouth.

But the puppet's lips might have been nailed together. They would not open.

In desperation the smaller of the two murderers pulled out a long knife from his pocket and tried to pry Pinocchio's mouth open with it.

Quick as a flash, the puppet sank his teeth deep into the murderer's hand. Fancy his surprise when he felt that it was not a hand, but a cat's paw.

He leaped away from the claws of these wicked ones and ran away across the fields. As he ran, the puppet felt more and more certain that he would have to give himself up into the hands of his pursuers. Suddenly he saw a little cottage among the trees of the forest. After a hard race, Pinocchio finally reached the door of the cottage and knocked. No one answered.

He knocked again, harder than before, for behind him he heard the steps of the murderers. Pinocchio, in despair, began to kick against the door as if he wanted to break it. At the noise, a window opened and a lovely maiden looked out. She had azure hair and a face as white as wax. Her eyes were closed and her hands crossed on her chest. She whispered: "No one lives in this house. Everyone is dead."

"Won't you, at least, open the door for me?" cried Pinocchio.

"I also am dead."

After these words, the girl disappeared and the window closed.

"Oh, Lovely Maiden with the Azure Hair," cried Pinocchio, "open, I beg of you. Take pity on a poor boy who is being chased by two—"

He did not finish, for two powerful hands grasped

him by the neck and the same two horrible voices growled: "Now we have you!"

They tied Pinocchio's hands behind his shoulders and slipped a noose around his neck. Throwing the rope over a high limb of a giant oak tree, they pulled till the poor puppet hung far up.

The murderers called to him: "Goodbye till tomorrow. When we return in the morning we hope you'll be polite enough to let us find you dead and gone and with your mouth wide open." With these words they went.

A few minutes went by and then a wild wind started to blow. As it shrieked and moaned the poor little puppet was blown to and fro like the hammer of a bell. The rocking made him seasick and the noose, becoming tighter, choked him.

V

The Field of Wonders

DEATH WAS CREEPING nearer and nearer. Luckily for Pinocchio, the Lovely Maiden with Azure Hair once again looked out of her window. Filled with pity at the sight of the poor little fellow being knocked about by the wind, she clapped her hands sharply together three times.

In moments, a large falcon came and settled itself on the window ledge. "What do you command, my charming Fairy?" asked the falcon.

The Lovely Maiden with the Azure Hair was none other than a very kind Fairy who had lived for more than a thousand years in this forest.

"Do you see that puppet hanging from the giant oak tree? Fly immediately to him. With your strong beak, break the knot which holds him tied, take him down, and lay him on the grass."

The falcon flew away and after two minutes returned, saying: "I have done what you have commanded."

The Fairy clapped her hands twice. A huge poodle appeared, walking on his hind legs just like a man.

"Come, Medoro," said the Fairy to him. "On reaching the oak tree, you will find a poor, half-dead puppet stretched out on the grass. Bring him here to me."

Medoro, to show that he understood, wagged his tail two or three times and set off.

In a short time the poodle returned with Pinocchio, and the Fairy, who was waiting at the door of the house, lifted the poor puppet in her arms and put him to bed. Touching him on the forehead, she noticed that he was burning with fever.

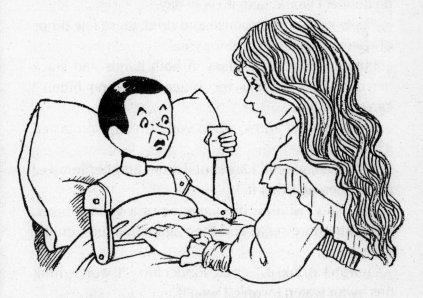

She took a glass of water, put a white powder into it and, handing it to the puppet, said, "Drink this, and in a few days you'll be up and well."

Pinocchio looked at the glass, made a sour face, and asked in a whining voice: "Is it sweet or bitter?"

"It is bitter, but it is good for you."

"If it is bitter, I don't want it."

"Drink it and I'll give you a lump of sugar to take the bitter taste from your mouth."

"I want the sugar first, then I'll drink the bitter water."

"Do you promise?"

"Yes."

The Fairy gave him the sugar and Pinocchio, after chewing and swallowing it, said, "If only sugar were medicine! I would take it every day."

"Now keep your promise and drink these few drops of water. They'll be good for you."

Pinocchio took the glass in both hands and stuck his nose into it. "It is too bitter, much too bitter! I can't drink it."

"How do you know, when you haven't even tasted it?"

"I can imagine it. I smell it. I want another lump of sugar, then I'll drink it."

The Fairy, with all the patience of a good mother, gave him more sugar and then again handed him the glass.

"I won't drink it," cried Pinocchio. "I won't drink this awful water. I won't, I won't!"

"In a few hours the fever will take you far away to another world."

"I don't care."

"Aren't you afraid of death?"

"Not a bit. I'd rather die than drink that awful medicine."

At that moment the door of the room flew open

and in came four black rabbits carrying a small black coffin on their shoulders.

"What do you want from me?" asked Pinocchio.

"We have come for you," said the largest rabbit.

"For me? But I'm not dead yet!"

"No, not dead yet; but you will be in a few moments since you have refused to take the medicine which would have made you well."

"Oh, Fairy, my Fairy," the puppet cried out, "give me that glass! Quick, please! I do not want to die!"

And holding the glass with his two hands, he swallowed the medicine at one gulp.

"Well," said the four rabbits, "this time we have made the trip for nothing."

In a twinkling Pinocchio felt fine. With one leap he was out of bed and into his clothes.

The Fairy, seeing him run and jump around the room, said "My medicine was good for you, after all, wasn't it?"

"Good indeed! It has given me new life."

"Why, then, did I have to beg you so hard to make you drink it?"

"I'm a boy, you see, and all boys hate medicine more than they do sickness."

"Come here now and tell me how it came about that you found yourself in the hands of the murderers."

And so Pinocchio told the Fairy with Azure Hair his whole long story ever since the time that Fire Eater gave him five gold pieces.

"Where are the gold pieces now?" the Fairy asked.

"I lost them," answered Pinocchio, but he told a lie, for he had them in his pocket.

As he spoke, his nose, long though it was, became at least two inches longer.

"And where did you lose them?"

"In the wood nearby."

At this second lie, his nose grew a few more inches.

"If you lost them in the nearby wood," said the Fairy, "we'll look for them and find them."

"Ah, now I remember," replied the puppet, becoming more and more confused, "I did not lose the gold pieces, but I swallowed them when I drank the medicine."

At his third lie, his nose became longer than ever, so long that he could not even turn around. If he turned to the right, he knocked it against the bed or into the windowpanes; if he turned to the left, he struck the walls or the door; if he raised it a bit, he almost put the Fairy's eyes out.

The Fairy sat looking at him and laughing.

"Why do you laugh?" the puppet asked her.

"I am laughing at your lies."

"How do you know I am lying?"

"Lies, my boy, are known in a moment. There are two kinds of lies. Lies with short legs and lies with long noses. Yours, just now, happen to have long noses."

Pinocchio, not knowing where to hide his shame, tried to escape from the room, but his nose had become so long that he could not get it out of the door.

The puppet cried for hours over the length of his nose. The Fairy was trying to teach him a lesson, so that he would stop telling lies, the worst habit any boy may have. But finally she began to feel sorry for him and clapped her hands together. A thousand woodpeckers flew in through the window and settled themselves on Pinocchio's nose. They pecked and pecked so hard at that enormous nose that, in a few minutes, it was the same size as before.

"How good you are, my Fairy," said Pinocchio, drying his eyes, "and how much I love you!"

"I love you, too," answered the Fairy, "and if you wish to stay with me, you may be my little brother and I'll be your good little sister."

"I should like to stay—but what about my poor father?"

"I have thought of everything. Your father has been sent for and before night he will be here."

"Really?" cried Pinocchio. "Then, my good Fairy, if you are willing, I should like to go to meet him. I cannot wait to kiss that dear old man, who has suffered so much for my sake."

"Surely, go ahead, but be careful not to lose your way. Take the forest path and you'll surely meet him."

Pinocchio set out, and as soon as he found himself in the wood, he ran like a rabbit. When he reached the giant oak tree he stopped, for he thought he heard a rustle in the brush. There stood the Fox and the Cat, his two traveling companions.

"Here comes our dear Pinocchio!" cried the Fox, hugging and kissing him. "How did you happen here?"

"It's a long story," said the Puppet. "But the other night, when you left me alone at the inn, I met murderers on the road—"

"Murderers? Oh, my poor friend! And what did they want?"

"They wanted my gold pieces."

"What an awful place to live in! Where shall we find a safe place for people like ourselves?"

As the Fox said this, Pinocchio noticed that the Cat carried his right paw in a sling.

"What happened to your paw?"

"It was caught in a trap," explained the Fox.

"In a trap," repeated the Cat.

"And what are you doing here?" the Fox asked the puppet.

"I am waiting for my father, who will be here at any moment."

"And your gold pieces?"

"I still have them in my pocket, except one which I spent at the Inn of the Red Lobster."

"Why don't you plant them in the Field of Wonders?"

"How far is it to this Field of Wonders?"

"Only two miles away. Will you come with us? We'll be there in half an hour. You can plant the money, and, after a few minutes, you will gather your two thousand coins and return home rich. Are you coming?"

Pinocchio hesitated a moment, for he remembered the good Fairy, old Geppetto and the advice of the Talking Cricket. Then he ended up by doing what all boys do when they have no heart and little brain. He shrugged his shoulders and said to the Fox and the Cat: "Let us go!"

And they went.

They walked and walked for half a day at least and at last they came to the town called the City of Simple Simons. As soon as they entered the town, Pinocchio noticed that all the streets were filled with hairless dogs, yawning from hunger; sheared sheep, trembling with cold; and plucked chickens, begging for a grain of wheat.

Through this crowd of beggars, beautiful horse-drawn coaches passed. Within them sat foxes, hawks and vultures.

Pinocchio, the Cat and the Fox passed through the city and, just outside the walls, they stepped into a lonely field, which looked more or less like any other field.

"Here we are," said the Fox to the puppet. "Dig a hole here and put the gold pieces into it."

The puppet obeyed. He dug the hole, put the four gold pieces into it and covered them up very carefully.

"Now," said the Fox, "go to that nearby stream, bring back a pail of water and sprinkle it over this spot."

Pinocchio followed the directions. Then he asked, "Anything else?"

"Nothing else," said the Fox. "Now we can go. Return here within twenty minutes and you will find the vine grown and the branches filled with gold pieces."

Pinocchio thanked the Fox and the Cat many times and promised them each a beautiful gift.

"We don't want any of your gifts," answered the two wicked ones. "It is enough for us that we have helped you to become rich with little or no trouble. For this we are as happy as kings."

They said goodbye to Pinocchio and, wishing him good luck, went on their way.

Minutes later the puppet returned to the field to see if, by any chance, a vine filled with gold coins was in sight. But he saw nothing! He went up to the place where he had dug the hole and buried the gold pieces. Again nothing!

He heard a burst of laughter close to his head. There, just above him on the branch of a tree, sat a large Parrot.

"What are you laughing at?"

"I am laughing at those simpletons who are so silly as to believe that gold can be planted in a field just like beans or squash. In order to come by money honestly, one must work and know how to earn it with hand or brain."

"I don't know what you are talking about," said the puppet.

"Too bad! I'll explain myself better. While you were in the city, the Fox and the Cat returned here in a great hurry. They took the four gold pieces which you had buried and ran away as fast as the wind."

Pinocchio's mouth opened wide. He would not believe the Parrot's words and began to dig at the earth. He dug and dug till the hole was as big as himself, but no money was there.

In desperation, he ran to the city and went straight to the courthouse to report the robbery to the judge.

The judge was a large, old gorilla.

Pinocchio, standing before him, told his pitiful story, word by word. He gave the names and the descriptions of the robbers and begged for justice.

The judge listened and a kind look shone in his eyes. He almost wept. When the puppet had no more to say, the judge put out his hand and rang a bell.

At the sound, two large dogs appeared, dressed in policemen's uniforms.

The judge said, pointing to Pinocchio, "This poor dumbbell has been robbed of four gold pieces. Take him and throw him into prison."

The puppet, on hearing this sentence, was shocked. He tried to protest, but the dogs led him away to jail.

There he had to remain for five long months. At that time, the young emperor of the City of Simple Simons had ordered a celebration for his victory over an enemy, and all the prisoners were set free.

Pinocchio ran out and away from that prison without looking back.

VI

Geppetto Is Lost at Sea

PINOCCHIO FLED from the city and set out on the road that was to take him back to the house of the lovely Fairy.

"How unhappy I have been," he said to himself. "And yet I deserve everything, for I am certainly very stubborn and stupid! I will always have my own way. I won't listen to those who love me and who have more brains than I. But from now on, I'll be different and I'll try to become a most obedient boy. I wonder if Father is waiting for me. Will I find him at the Fairy's house? And will the Fairy ever forgive me for all I have done? Can there be a worse or more heartless boy than I am anywhere?"

Pinocchio started to run across the fields and meadows, and never stopped till he came to the main road that was to take him to the Fairy's house.

He finally came to the spot where the house once stood, but the little house was no longer there. In its place lay a small marble slab, which bore these sad words:

HERE LIES

THE LOVELY FAIRY WITH AZURE HAIR

WHO DIED OF GRIEF

WHEN

ABANDONED

BY

HER LITTLE BROTHER PINOCCHIO

The poor puppet was heartbroken at reading these words. He fell to the ground and burst into tears. As he sobbed he said to himself: "Oh, my Fairy, my dear, dear Fairy, why did you die? Why did not I die, who am so bad, instead of you, who are so good? And my father—where can he be? Please, dear Fairy, tell me where he is and I shall never, never leave him again! You are not really dead, are you? If you love me, you will come back, alive as before."

Poor Pinocchio! He even tried to tear his hair, but as it was only painted on his wooden head, he could not even pull it.

Just then a large Pigeon flew far above him. Seeing the puppet, he cried to him: "Tell me, little boy, do you by chance know of a puppet, Pinocchio by name?"

"Pinocchio! Why, I am Pinocchio!"

At this answer the Pigeon flew down to the earth. He was much larger than a turkey.

"Then you know Geppetto also?"

"He's my father! Will you take me to him? Is he still alive?"

"I left him three days ago on the shore of a large sea," said the Pigeon. "He was building a little boat with which to cross the ocean. For the last four months, that poor man has been wandering around Europe, looking for you. Not having found you yet, he has made up his mind to look for you in the New World, far across the ocean."

"Oh, dear Pigeon," said Pinocchio, "how I wish I had your wings!"

"If you want to come, I'll take you with me, astride my back."

Pinocchio jumped on the Pigeon's back, the bird flew away, and in a few minutes they had reached the clouds. They flew all day, they flew all night. The next morning they were at the seashore.

Pinocchio jumped off the Pigeon's back, and the Pigeon, not wanting any thanks for a kind deed, flew away swiftly and disappeared.

The shore was full of people, shrieking and tearing their hair as they looked toward the sea.

"What has happened?" asked Pinocchio of a little old woman.

"A poor old father lost his only son some time ago and today he built a tiny boat for himself in order to go in search for him across the ocean. The water is very rough and we are afraid he will be drowned."

Pinocchio looked out and saw in the distance a tiny shadow, no bigger than a nutshell, floating on the sea.

"It's my father! It's my father!"

Meanwhile, the little boat, tossed about by the angry waves, appeared and disappeared. Pinocchio, standing on a high rock, waved to him with hand and cap and even with his nose.

It looked as if Geppetto, though far away from the shore, recognized his son, for he took off his cap and waved also. He seemed to be trying to make everyone understand that he would come back if he were able, but the sea was so heavy that he could do nothing with his oars. Suddenly a huge wave came and the boat disappeared.

They waited and waited for it, but it was gone.

"Poor man!" said the fisher folk on the shore, whispering a prayer as they turned to go home.

"I'll save him!" cried Pinocchio, "I'll save my father!"

Pinocchio dove into the sea. Being made of wood, he floated easily along and swam like a fish in the rough water. Now and again he disappeared only to reappear once more. At last he was lost to view.

"Poor boy!" cried the fisher folk, and again they mumbled a few prayers as they returned home.

Pinocchio swam all night long but could not find his father. At dawn he saw, not far away, a long stretch of sand. It was an island in the middle of the sea.

He swam to it and from there looked over the water to see whether he might catch sight of a boat with a little man in it. He searched and searched, but he saw nothing except the sea and sky. Finally, he saw a big fish swimming nearby, with his head far out of the water.

Not knowing what to call him, the puppet said, "Hey, there, Mr. Fish, may I have a word with you?"

"Even two, if you want," answered the fish, who happened to be a very polite Dolphin.

"Did you not perhaps meet a little boat with my father in it?"

"In the storm of last night," answered the Dolphin, "the little boat must have been swamped."

"And my father?"

"By this time, he must have been swallowed by the terrible Shark, which, for the last few days, has been bringing terror to these waters. Just to give you an idea of his size, let me tell you that he is larger than a five-story building and that he has a mouth so big and so deep that a whole train and engine could easily get into it."

"Oh no!" cried the puppet, scared to death. "Farewell, Mr. Fish. Many thanks for your kindness."

This said, he took the path behind him, but at every sound he turned to see whether the terrible Shark, five stories high and with a train in his mouth, was following him.

After walking half an hour, he came to a small country called the Land of the Busy Bees. The streets were filled with people running to and fro about their tasks. Everyone worked, everyone had something to do.

"This is no place for me," said Pinocchio. "I was not born to work."

But he began to feel hungry, for it was a day since he had eaten. What was to be done? There were only two ways left to him in order to get a bite to eat. He had either to work or to beg.

He was ashamed to beg, because his father had told him that begging should be done only by the sick or the old. He had said that the real poor in this world, deserving of our pity and our help, were only those who, either through age or sickness, had lost the means of earning their bread with their own hands.

Just then a man passed by, pulling two heavy carts filled with coal.

Pinocchio looked at him and said with eyes downcast in shame: "Will you be so good as to give me a penny, for I am faint with hunger."

"Not only one penny," said the coal man. "I'll give you four if you will help me pull these two wagons."

"I wish you to know," said the puppet, very much offended, "that I never have been a donkey, nor have I ever pulled a wagon."

"Then, my boy, if you are really faint with hunger, eat two slices of your pride, and I hope they don't give you a stomachache."

A few minutes later a bricklayer passed by, carrying a pail full of plaster on his shoulder.

"Good man, will you be kind enough to give a penny to a poor boy who is hungry?"

"Gladly," answered the bricklayer. "Come with me and carry some plaster, and instead of one penny I'll give you five."

"But the plaster is heavy," said Pinocchio, "and the work too hard for me."

"If the work is too hard for you, my boy, enjoy your hunger."

In less than half an hour, at least twenty people passed and Pinocchio begged of each one, but they all answered: "Aren't you ashamed? Instead of being a beggar in the streets, why don't you look for work and earn your own bread?"

Finally a little woman went by carrying two water jugs.

"Good woman, will you allow me to have a drink from one of your jugs?" asked Pinocchio.

"With pleasure, my boy!" she answered.

When Pinocchio had had his fill, he grumbled as he wiped his mouth, "My thirst is gone. If I could only as easily get rid of my hunger."

On hearing these words, the good little woman said, "If you help me to carry these jugs home, I'll give you a slice of bread."

Pinocchio looked at the jug and said neither yes nor no.

"And with the bread I'll give you a nice dish of cauliflower with white sauce on it."

Pinocchio gave the jug another look and said neither yes nor no.

"And after the cauliflower, some cake and jam."

At these last items, he could no longer resist and said, "Very well. I'll take the jug home for you."

The jug was very heavy, and the puppet, not being strong enough to carry it with his hands, had to put it on his head.

VII

Pinocchio Is Arrested

W HEN THEY ARRIVED HOME, the little woman
made Pinocchio sit down at a small table and
placed before him the bread, the cauliflower and the
cake. He devoured them all.

When his hunger was satisfied, he raised his head
to thank this kind woman. But he had not looked at
her long when he gave a cry of surprise and sat there
with his eyes wide open.

"Why all the surprise?" asked the woman.

"Because—" answered Pinocchio, "because—you
look like—you remind me of—yes, yes, the same
voice, the same eyes, the same hair—yes, yes, yes,
you also have the same azure hair she had! Oh, my
little Fairy, my little Fairy! Tell me that it is you! Don't
make me cry any longer!"

And Pinocchio threw himself on the floor and clasped her knees. If he cried much longer the little woman thought he would melt away, so she finally admitted that she was the little Fairy with Azure Hair.

"You rascal of a puppet, how did you know it was I?" she asked, laughing.

"My love for you told me who you were."

"Do you remember? You left me when I was a little girl and now you find me a grown woman. I am so old, I could almost be your mother!"

"I am very glad of that, for then I can call you Mother instead of Sister. For a long time I have wanted a mother, just like other boys. But how did you grow so quickly?"

"That's a secret!"

"Tell it to me. I also want to grow a little. Look at me! I have never grown higher than a block of cheese."

"But you can't grow," answered the Fairy.

"Why not?"

"Because puppets never grow. They are born puppets, they live puppets and they die puppets."

"Oh, I'm tired of always being a puppet!" cried Pinocchio. "It's about time I grew into a man as everyone else does."

"And you will if you deserve it—"

"Really? What can I do to deserve it?"

"It's a very simple matter. Try to act like a well-behaved child."

"Don't you think I do?"

"Far from it! Good boys are obedient, and you, on the contrary—"

"And I never obey."

"Good boys love study and work, but you—"

"And I, on the contrary, am a lazy fellow."

"Good boys always tell the truth."

"And I always tell lies."

"Good boys go gladly to school."

"And I get sick if I go to school. From now on it'll be different."

"Do you promise?"

"I promise. I want to become a good boy and be a comfort to my father. Where is my poor father now?"

"I do not know."

"Will I ever be lucky enough to find him and embrace him once more?"

"I think so. Indeed, I am sure of it."

At this answer, Pinocchio's happiness was very great. "Tell me, little Mother, it isn't true that you are dead, is it?"

"It doesn't seem so," answered the Fairy.

"If you only knew how I suffered and how I wept when I read: 'Here lies—' "

"I know it, and for that I have forgiven you. The depth of your sorrow made me see that you have a kind heart. There is always hope for boys with hearts such as yours, though they often seem very mischievous. This is the reason I have come so far to look for you. From now on, I'll be your own little mother."

"Oh! How lovely!" cried Pinocchio.

"You will always obey me and do as I wish?"

"Gladly!"

"Beginning tomorrow," said the Fairy, "you'll go to school every day."

Pinocchio's face fell a little.

"Then you will choose the trade you like best."

"But I don't want either a trade or profession. Work wearies me!"

"My dear boy," said the Fairy, "people who speak as you do usually end their days in a prison or a hospital. A man, remember, whether rich or poor, should do something in this world. No one can find happiness without work."

These words touched Pinocchio's heart. "I'll work; I'll study! I'll do all you tell me. After all, the life of a puppet has grown very tiresome to me and I want to become a boy, no matter how hard it is. You promise that, do you not?"

"Yes, I promise, and now it is up to you."

In the morning, Pinocchio started for school.

As the days passed into weeks, the teacher praised Pinocchio, for he saw him attentive, hardworking and wide-awake. The puppet's only fault was that he had too many friends. Among these were many rascals, who didn't care a bit for studying.

The teacher warned him each day, and even the good Fairy repeated to him many times: "Take care, Pinocchio! Those bad companions will sooner or later make you lose your love for study. Some day they will lead you astray."

"There's no such danger," answered the puppet. "I'm too wise for that to happen."

But one day, as he was walking to school, he met some boys who ran up to him and said, "Have you heard the news? A Shark as big as a mountain has been seen near the shore."

"Really? I wonder if it could be the same one I heard of when my father was drowned."

"We are going to the shore to see it. Are you coming?"

"No, not I. I must go to school."

"What do you care about school? You can go there tomorrow. With a lesson more or less, we are always the same donkeys."

"For certain reasons of my own, I, too, want to see that Shark! But I'll go after school."

"Poor dope!" cried one boy. "Do you think a fish of that size will stand there waiting for you?"

"Very well, then," said Pinocchio. "Let's see who gets there first!" The little troop, with books under their arms, dashed across the fields.

When they reached the shore, the sea was as smooth as glass. "Where's that Shark?" asked Pinocchio.

From the answers and laughter that followed, Pinocchio understood that the boys had played a trick on him.

"What's the joke?" he asked.

"That we have made you stay out of school to come with us. Aren't you ashamed of being such a

goody-two-shoes and of studying so hard? You never have a bit of fun."

"And what is it to you if I do study?"

"Don't you see? If you study and we don't, we pay for it."

"What do you want me to do?"

"Hate school and books and teachers, as we all do."

"And if I go on studying, what will you do to me?"

"You'll pay for it."

"Cuckoo!" said the puppet, mocking them with his thumb to his nose.

"You'll be sorry!"

"Cuckoo!"

"Very well, then! Take that!" And the boldest of the seven other boys gave Pinocchio a terrible blow on the head.

Pinocchio returned that blow and in a few moments the fight raged.

Pinocchio, although alone, defended himself bravely. With those two wooden feet of his, he worked so fast that his opponents kept at a distance. Enraged at not being able to fight the puppet up close, they started to throw all kinds of books at him.

When the boys had used all their own books, they looked around for new ammunition. Seeing Pinocchio's bundle lying nearby, they picked it up. One of Pinocchio's books was a very large volume of arithmetic. It was Pinocchio's favorite.

Thinking it would make a good missile, one of the boys took hold of it and threw it with all his strength at Pinocchio's head. But instead of hitting the puppet, the book struck Eugene, one of the other boys, who fell senseless to the ground.

At the sight of that accident, the other boys were so frightened that they turned and ran. All except Pinocchio.

Although scared, he ran to the sea and soaked his handkerchief in the cool water and with it bathed the head of his poor little schoolmate. "Eugene! My poor Eugene! Open your eyes and look at me!" he said aloud. And to himself he said, "Oh, how much better it would have been, if only I had gone to school! Why did I listen to those boys? And to think that the teacher had told me—and my mother had told me, too! 'Beware of bad company!' But I'm stubborn and though I listen, always I do as I wish. And then I pay. I've never had a moment's peace since I've been born! What will become of me?"

Pinocchio went on crying and beating his head. Again and again he called to his little friend, when suddenly he heard heavy steps approaching. He looked up and saw two police officers.

"Who has hurt this boy?" asked one.

"Not I," stammered the puppet.

"And with what was he wounded?"

"With this book," said the puppet.

"And whose book is this?"

"Mine."

"Enough! Get up as quickly as you can and come with us."

"But I . . . but I am innocent."

Before starting out the officers called out to several fishermen and said to them, "Take care of this little boy who has been hurt."

They then took hold of Pinocchio and marched with him along the road to the village.

They had just reached the village when a sudden gust of wind blew off Pinocchio's cap and made it go sailing far down the street.

"Would you allow me to run after my cap?" Pinocchio asked the officers.

"Very well, but hurry."

The puppet went, picked up his cap—and then raced toward the sea. He went like a bullet out of a gun.

The officers, seeing that it would be very difficult to catch him, let him go.

VIII

Pinocchio Leaves with Lampwick

WHEN PINOCCHIO GOT NEAR the shore he passed by a little hut, where an old man sat at the door sunning himself. Pinocchio asked, "Tell me, good man, have you heard anything of a poor boy with a wounded head, whose name was Eugene?"

"The boy was brought to this hut and now—"

"Now he is dead?"

"No, he is alive and he has already returned home."

"Really? Really?" cried the puppet, jumping around with joy. "Then the wound was not serious?"

"But it might have been," answered the old man. "For a heavy book was thrown at his head by a schoolmate of his, a certain Pinocchio."

"And who is this Pinocchio?" asked the puppet, pretending he didn't know.

"They say he is a mischief maker, a no-good, a street boy—"

"Lies! All lies!"

"Do you know this Pinocchio? What do you think of him?"

"I think he's a very good boy, fond of study, obedient, kind to his father, and to his whole family—"

As he was telling these enormous lies about himself, Pinocchio touched his nose and found it twice as long as it should be. Scared out of his wits, he cried out: "Don't listen to me, good man! All the wonderful things I have said are not true at all. I know Pinocchio well and he is indeed a very wicked boy, lazy and disobedient, who, instead of going to school, runs away with his friends to have a good time."

At this speech his nose returned to its natural size.

And now he went on his way back to the village. He was so worried, however, that he went along taking two steps forward and one back, saying to himself, "How shall I ever face my good little Fairy? What will she say when she sees me? I am a rascal, fine on promises which I never keep!"

He came to the village late at night. It was raining and pouring. He was too ashamed to knock at the door and face the Fairy, so he crawled under a ledge out of the rain and shivered away the rest of the night until he fell asleep.

The next thing he knew he was stretched out on a sofa and the Fairy was seated near him.

"This time I will forgive you," said the Fairy to him.

"But be careful not to get into mischief again."

Pinocchio promised to study and behave himself. And he kept his word for the remainder of the year. At the end of it, he passed first in all his examinations, and his report card was so good that the Fairy said to him, "Tomorrow your wish will come true. Tomorrow you will cease to be a puppet and will become a real boy."

Pinocchio was beside himself with joy. All his friends and schoolmates must be invited to celebrate the great event! The Fairy promised to prepare a party for the next day.

Pinocchio went out to invite his friends. Now it must be known that, among all his friends, Pinocchio had one whom he loved most of all. The boy's name was Lampwick. Lampwick was the laziest boy in the school and the biggest mischief maker.

Pinocchio searched here and there and everywhere for his friend, and finally discovered him near a farmer's wagon.

"What are you doing there?" asked Pinocchio.

"I am waiting for midnight to strike to go far, far away!"

"Haven't you heard the news? Tomorrow I end my days as a puppet and become a boy, like you and all my other friends. Will I see you at my party tomorrow?"

"But I'm telling you that I go tonight. To a real country—the best in the world—a wonderful place! It is called the Land of Toys. Why don't you come, too?"

"I? Oh, no."

"Believe me, if you don't come, you'll be sorry. No schools, no teachers, no books! In the Land of Toys, every day is a Saturday. Vacation begins on the first of January and ends on the last day of December. Days are spent in play and enjoyment from morning till night. At night one goes to bed, and next morning good times begin all over again. What do you think of it? Do you want to go with me, then?"

"No, no, and again no! I have promised my kind Fairy to become a good boy, and I want to keep my word. The sun is setting and I must leave you and run. My good Fairy wants me to return home before night. Goodbye and good luck to you!"

"Wait two minutes more."

"And if the good Fairy scolds me?"

"Let her scold. After she gets tired, she will stop," said Lampwick. "At midnight the wagon passes here that is to take us within the boundaries of that marvelous country. Why don't you come, too?"

"It is useless for you to tempt me! I promised the good Fairy to behave myself, and I am going to keep my word."

"Goodbye, then, and remember me while you're in grammar school, and high school and even in college."

"Goodbye, Lampwick. Have a pleasant trip.—And how soon is it that you go?"

"Within two hours."

"I might wait with you."

"And the Fairy?"

"By this time I'm late, and an hour or two more or less makes very little difference."

"And if the Fairy scolds you?"

"Oh, I'll let her scold," said Pinocchio. "After she gets tired, she will stop."

The night became darker and darker. All at once in the distance a small light flickered.

"There it is!" cried Lampwick. "The wagon that is coming to get me. For the last time, are you coming or not?"

"But is it really true that in that country boys never have to study?"

"Never, never, never!"

The wagon arrived. It was drawn by twelve pairs of donkeys, all of the same size, but all of different colors. Some were gray, others white, and still others a mixture of brown and black.

The strangest thing of all was that those twenty-four donkeys had on their feet laced shoes made of leather, just like the ones boys wear.

And the driver of the wagon?

Just imagine a little, fat man, much wider than he was long, round and shiny as a ball of butter, with a face beaming like an apple, a little mouth that always smiled and a voice like that of a cat begging for food.

The wagon was so closely packed with boys of all ages that it looked like a box of sardines. The thought that in a few hours they would reach a country where there were no schools, no books, no teachers, made these boys so happy that they felt neither hunger, nor thirst, nor sleep nor discomfort.

No sooner had the wagon stopped than the little fat man turned to Lampwick. He asked, "Tell me, my fine boy, do you also want to come to my wonderful country?"

"Indeed I do."

With one leap Lampwick perched himself on top of the coach.

"What about you, my boy?" asked the little man of Pinocchio. "Will you come with us, or do you stay here?"

"I stay here," said Pinocchio. "I want to return home, as I prefer to study and to succeed in life."

"Pinocchio!" Lampwick called out. "Come with us and we'll always be happy."

"No, no, no!"

"Come with us and we'll always be happy!" cried four other voices from the wagon.

"Come with us and we'll always be happy!" shouted the one hundred and more boys in the wagon.

Pinocchio sighed deeply once—twice—a third time. Finally he said, "Make room for me. I want to go, too!"

Pinocchio mounted a donkey and the wagon started on its way. While the donkeys galloped along the stony road, the puppet fancied he heard a very quiet voice whispering to him: "Poor silly! You are going to be a sorry boy before very long."

Pinocchio looked about to see from where the words had come, but he saw no one. The donkeys galloped, the wagon rolled on, the boys slept, and the little, fat driver watched.

After a mile or so, Pinocchio again heard the same faint voice whispering: "Remember, dumbbell! Boys who stop studying and turn their backs upon books and schools and teachers in order to give all their time to nonsense and pleasure, sooner or later find trouble. Oh, how well I know this! A day will come when you will weep bitterly, even as I am weeping now—but it will be too late!"

The puppet jumped to the ground, ran up to the donkey on whose back he had been riding. How great was his surprise when he saw that the donkey was weeping—weeping just like a boy!

"Come, come," called out the driver, "do not lose sleep over a donkey that can weep. Get back on and let us go. The night is cool and the road is long."

Pinocchio obeyed. The wagon started again. Toward dawn the next morning they reached the Land of Toys.

IX

Life as a Donkey

THIS GREAT LAND WAS entirely different from any other place in the world. Its population was composed wholly of boys. The oldest were about fourteen years of age, the youngest, eight. Everywhere groups of boys played together. All together they created such a ruckus that it would have been necessary for you to put cotton in your ears.

As soon as they had set foot in this land, Pinocchio, Lampwick and all the other boys who had traveled with them started out on a tour. They wandered everywhere. They became everybody's friend. Who could be happier than they?

What with games and parties, the hours, the days, the weeks passed like lightning.

"Oh, what a beautiful life this is!" said Pinocchio each time that he met his friend Lampwick.

"Was I right or wrong?" asked Lampwick. "And to think you did not want to come!"

Five months passed by and the boys continued playing and enjoying themselves from morning till night, without ever seeing a book, or a desk or a school. But there came a morning when Pinocchio awoke and found a great surprise awaiting him.

On awakening, Pinocchio put his hand up to his head and there he found—

Guess!

He found that, during the night, his ears had grown at least ten full inches!

He went in search of a mirror, but not finding any, he just filled a basin with water and looked at himself. There he saw what he never could have wished to see. He began to cry, to scream, to knock his head against the wall, but the more he shrieked, the longer and more hairy grew his ears.

At hearing these shrieks, a dormouse came into the room, a fat little dormouse, who lived upstairs.

She took the puppet's hand and said, "You have donkey fever. Within two or three hours, you will no longer be a puppet, nor a boy."

"What shall I be?"

"A real donkey, just like the ones that pull the fruit carts to market. Fate has ordered that all lazy boys who come to hate books and schools and teachers and spend all their days with toys and games must sooner or later turn into donkeys."

"But the fault is not mine, little dormouse, the fault is all Lampwick's! I wanted to return home, I wanted to be obedient, but Lampwick said to me, 'Why do you want to waste your time studying? Come with me to the Land of Toys.' "

"And why did you follow the advice of that false friend?"

"Why? Because I am a thoughtless and heartless puppet!"

When Pinocchio went to Lampwick's room to scold his friend, there was another surprise. Each of them had grown these silly donkey ears, and, instead of feeling sorrowful and ashamed, they burst into laughter! They laughed and laughed till they cried.

But all of a sudden Lampwick stopped laughing. He stumbled and almost fell. "Help, help, Pinocchio! I can no longer stand up."

"I can't either!" cried Pinocchio; and his laughter turned to tears as they both fell on all fours and began running and jumping around the room. As they ran, their arms turned into legs, their faces lengthened into snouts and their backs became covered with long gray hairs.

The most horrible moment was the one in which the two poor creatures felt their tails appear. They tried to cry, but instead of moans and cries, they burst forth into loud donkey brays, which sounded very much like, "Haw! Haw! Haw!"

At that moment a loud knocking was heard at the door and a voice called to them: "Open up!" It was the little man who had driven them to the Land of Toys. He kicked the door open, looked at Pinocchio and Lampwick, and said, "You have brayed well!"

The two donkeys bowed their heads in shame. Their ears drooped and they put their tails between their legs.

At first the little man petted them and smoothed down their hairy coats. Then he took out a horse brush and worked them over till they shone like glass. He then bridled them and took them to a marketplace far away from the Land of Toys, in the hope of selling them at a good price.

Lampwick was bought by a farmer whose donkey had died the day before. Pinocchio went to the owner of a circus, who wanted to teach him to do tricks for his audiences.

And now do you understand what the little man's profession was? This horrid little being, whose face shone with kindness, went about the world looking for boys. Lazy boys, boys who hated books, boys who wanted to run away from home—all these were his joy and fortune. He took them with him to the Land of Toys and let them enjoy themselves to their heart's content. When, after months of all play and no work,

they became little donkeys, he sold them on the marketplace. In a few years he had become a millionaire.

After putting Pinocchio in a stable, his new master filled his manger with straw, but Pinocchio, after tasting a mouthful, spat it out.

"Do you think, perhaps, my little donkey," said his master, "that I have brought you here only to give you food and drink? Oh, no! You are to help me earn some fine gold pieces. I am going to teach you to jump and bow, to dance, and even to stand on your head."

Poor Pinocchio, whether he liked it or not, had to learn all these things; but it took him three long months and cost him many, many lashings before he was pronounced perfect.

The day came at last when Pinocchio's master was able to announce an extraordinary performance featuring Pinocchio, the dancing donkey. The theater was filled to overflowing.

"Ready, Pinocchio!" said the master. "Before starting your performance, salute your audience!"

Pinocchio bent his two knees to the ground and remained kneeling until the master, with the crack of a whip, cried, "Walk!"

The donkey lifted himself on his four feet and walked around the ring. Then the master called, "Quickstep!" and Pinocchio changed his step.

"Gallop!" and Pinocchio galloped.

"Full speed!" and Pinocchio ran as fast as he could. As he ran the master raised his arm and a pistol shot rang in the air.

At the shot, the little donkey fell to the ground as if he were really dead.

A shower of applause greeted the donkey as he arose to his feet. At that noise, Pinocchio lifted his head and raised his eyes. There, in front of him, in the audience, sat a beautiful woman. Around her neck she wore a long gold chain, from which hung a huge medallion. On the medallion was painted the picture of a puppet.

"That picture is of me! That beautiful lady is my Fairy!" said Pinocchio. But instead of words, a loud braying was heard in the theater, and all the spectators burst out laughing.

Then, in order to teach the donkey that it was not good manners to bray before the public, the master hit him on the nose with the handle of his whip.

The poor little donkey stuck out a long tongue and licked his nose for a long time in an effort to take away the pain.

And what was his grief when, on looking up toward the audience, he saw that the Fairy had disappeared.

He felt himself fainting, his eyes filled with tears, and he wept.

"Now," said the master, "show us how you can jump through a ring."

As he leaped through, his hind legs caught in the ring and he fell to the floor in a heap.

When he got up, he was lame and could hardly limp as far as the stable.

The next morning the animal doctor declared that he would be lame for the rest of his life.

"What do I want with a lame donkey?" said the master to the stable boy. "Take him to the market and sell him."

The boy did so, and sold him for four cents to an old musician who wanted the donkey's skin to make himself a drumhead.

Pinocchio's new owner took him to a high cliff overlooking the sea, put a stone around his neck, tied a rope to one of his hind feet, gave him a push, and threw him into the water.

Pinocchio sank down into the sea, deeper and

deeper, and his new master sat on the cliff waiting for him to drown, so as to skin him and make himself a drumhead.

After an hour, the master pulled the rope which he had tied to Pinocchio's leg, and pulled and pulled and pulled, and, at last, he saw appear on the surface of the water—can you guess what? Instead of a dead donkey, he saw a very much alive puppet, wriggling and squirming like an eel!

"How is it that you, who a few minutes ago were a donkey, are now standing before me a wooden puppet?"

"My Fairy takes care of me," answered Pinocchio. "Like all other mothers who love their children, she never loses sight of me, even though I do not deserve it. And today this good Fairy of mine, as soon as she saw me in danger of drowning, sent a thousand fishes to the spot where I lay. They thought I was a dead donkey and began to eat me. What great bites they took! One ate my ears, another my nose, a third my neck and my mane. Some went at my legs and some at my back, and among the others, there was one tiny fish so gentle and polite that he did me the great favor of eating even my tail. When the fish finished eating my donkey coat, they naturally came to the bones—or rather, in my case, to the wood. After the first few bites, those fish found out that the wood was not good for their teeth, and, afraid of indigestion, they turned and left. Now you know why you found a puppet and not a dead donkey when you pulled me out of the water."

"I spent four cents on you, and I want my money back!" said the musician. "I am going to take you to the market once more and sell you as firewood."

Pinocchio laughed and gave a quick leap and dived into the sea. Swimming away as fast as he could, he cried out, "Goodbye, master."

In a few seconds he had gone so far he could hardly be seen. After swimming for a long time, Pinocchio saw a large rock in the middle of the sea. High on the rock stood a little Goat bleating and calling to the puppet to come to her.

There was something very strange about that little Goat. Her coat was not white or black or brown, but azure, a color that reminded him of the hair of the lovely maiden.

Pinocchio's heart beat fast as he swam as hard as he could toward the white rock. Suddenly, a horrible sea monster stuck its head out of the water. The sea monster was none other than the enormous Shark!

Poor Pinocchio! He tried to swim away from the Shark, to change his path, to escape, but that immense mouth kept coming nearer and nearer.

"Hurry, Pinocchio, I beg you!" bleated the little Goat on the high rock.

And Pinocchio swam faster and faster, and harder and harder.

"There he is," cried the Goat. "Quick, quick, or you are lost!" The Goat leaned over to give him one of her hoofs to help him up out of the water.

Alas! It was too late! The monster overtook him and the puppet found himself in between the rows of gleaming white teeth. Only for a moment, however, for the Shark took a deep breath and, as he breathed, he drank in the puppet as easily as he would have sucked an egg.

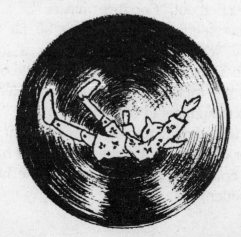

X

The Family Reunited

WHEN PINOCCHIO RECOVERED his senses, he could not remember where he was. Around him all was darkness. He listened for a few moments and heard nothing. Once in a while a cold wind blew on his face. The Shark was suffering from asthma, so that whenever he breathed a storm seemed to blow.

As soon as Pinocchio realized he was really and truly in the Shark's stomach, he cried, "Help! Won't someone come save me?"

After a few moments Pinocchio thought he saw a faint light in the distance. As he walked toward the light, his feet splashed in a pool of greasy and slippery water. The further on he went, the brighter and clearer grew the tiny light. On and on he walked till finally he found—I give you a thousand guesses! He found a little table set for dinner and lighted by a candle stuck in a glass bottle; and near the table sat a little old man.

At this sight, the poor puppet was filled with such great and sudden happiness that he almost dropped in a faint. He wanted to laugh, he wanted to cry. "Oh, Father, dear Father! Have I found you at last?"

"Are my eyes really telling me the truth?" answered the old man. "Are you really my own dear Pinocchio?"

"Yes, yes, yes! It is I! You have forgiven me, haven't you, Father?" Pinocchio told Geppetto the story of his two years of adventures and sorrows, and then Pinocchio asked, "How have you lived, Father? Where did you find the candle and matches?"

"In the storm that swamped my boat, dear son, a large ship also suffered the same fate. The sailors were all saved, but the ship went right to the bottom of the sea and the same terrible Shark that swallowed me swallowed most of it."

"What! Swallowed a ship?"

"At one gulp. To my own good luck, that ship was loaded with meat, preserved foods, crackers, bread, bottles of wine, raisins, cheese, coffee, sugar, wax candles and boxes of matches. With all these blessings, I have been able to live happily on, for two whole years, but now I am at the very last crumbs. Today there is nothing left in the cupboard, and this candle you see here is the last one I have."

"Then, my dear father," said Pinocchio, "there is no time to lose. We must try to escape. We can run out of the Shark's mouth and dive into the sea."

"I cannot swim, my dear Pinocchio."

"You can climb on my shoulders and I, who am a fine swimmer, will carry you safely to shore. Follow me and have no fear."

They walked a long distance through the stomach and the whole body of the Shark. When they reached the throat of the monster, they stopped for a while to wait for the right moment in which to make their escape.

The Shark, being very old and suffering from asthma and heart trouble, was obliged to sleep with his mouth open.

They climbed up the throat of the monster till they came to that immense open mouth. There they had to walk on tiptoes, for if they tickled the Shark's long tongue he might awaken—and where would they be then? But before they took the last great leap, the puppet said to his father: "Climb on my back and hold on tightly to my neck. I'll take care of everything else."

As soon as Geppetto was seated on his shoulders, Pinocchio dived into the water and started to swim. The sea was like oil, the moon shone and the Shark continued to sleep so soundly that not even a cannon shot would have awakened him.

As soon as they reached the shore, Pinocchio offered his arm to Geppetto, who was so weak he could hardly stand.

"Lean on my arm, dear Father, and let us go. We shall walk very, very slowly." They had not taken a hundred steps when they saw two rough-looking individuals sitting on a stone begging for pennies.

It was the Fox and the Cat. The Cat, after pretending to be blind for so many years, had really lost the sight in both eyes. And the Fox, old, thin and almost hairless, had even lost his tail.

"Oh, Pinocchio," cried the Fox, "give us some money, we beg you! We are old, tired and sick."

"Sick!" repeated the Cat.

"If you are poor and sick, you deserve it! Remember the old proverb that says: 'Stolen money never bears fruit.' Goodbye, false friends."

"Do not abandon us."

Waving goodbye to them, Pinocchio and Geppetto went on their way. After a few more steps, they saw, at the end of a long road near a clump of trees, a tiny cottage built of straw.

They went and knocked at the door.

"Who is it?" said a little voice from within.

"A poor father and a poorer son, without food and with no roof to cover them," answered the puppet.

"Turn the key and the door will open," said the voice.

As soon as they went in, they looked here and there and everywhere but saw no one.

"Here I am, up here!"

Father and son looked up to the ceiling, and there on a beam sat the Talking Cricket.

"Oh, my dear Cricket," said Pinocchio.

"Oh, now you call me your dear Cricket, but do you remember when you threw your hammer at me to kill me?"

"You are right, dear Cricket. Throw a hammer at me now. I deserve it! But spare my poor old father."

"I am going to spare both father and son. I have only wanted to remind you of the trick you long ago played upon me, to teach you that in this world of ours we must be kind and courteous to others, if we want to find kindness and courtesy in our own days of trouble."

"You are right, little Cricket, and I will remember the lesson you have taught me. But will you tell me how you bought this pretty little cottage?"

"It was given to me yesterday by a little Goat with blue hair. Yesterday she went away bleating sadly, and it seemed to me she said: 'Poor Pinocchio, I shall never see him again . . . the Shark must have eaten him.' "

"Then it was she—it was—my dear little Fairy," cried out Pinocchio, sobbing.

After he had cried a long time, he wiped his eyes and made a bed of straw for old Geppetto. He laid him on it and said to the Talking Cricket: "Tell me, little Cricket, where shall I find a glass of milk for my poor father?"

"Three fields away there lives Farmer John. He has

some cows. Go there and he will give you what you want."

Pinocchio ran all the way to Farmer's John's house. The farmer said, "How much milk do you want?"

"I want a full glass."

"A full glass costs a penny. First give me the penny."

"I have no penny," answered Pinocchio.

"Very bad, my puppet," answered the farmer, "very bad. If you have no penny, I have no milk. But perhaps we can come to terms. Do you know how to draw water from a well?"

"I can try."

"Then go to that well and draw one hundred bucketfuls of water. After you have finished, I shall give you a glass of warm sweet milk."

By the time he was finished pulling up the one hundred bucketfuls, Pinocchio knew he had never worked so hard in his life.

"Until today," said the farmer, "my donkey has drawn the water for me, but now that poor animal is dying."

"Will you take me to see him?" said Pinocchio.

"Gladly."

As soon as Pinocchio went into the stable, he saw a little donkey lying on a bed of straw. He was worn out from hunger and too much work. After looking at him, the puppet said to himself, "I know that donkey!"

He bent low over him and asked, "Who are you?"

At this question, the donkey opened his weary eyes and answered, "I am Lampwick."

Then he closed his eyes and died!

"Oh, my poor Lampwick!"

The farmer then gave Pinocchio the glass of milk and the puppet took it and returned to his father.

From that day on, for more than five months, Pinocchio got up every morning just as dawn was breaking and went to the farm to draw water. And every day he was given a glass of warm milk for his poor old father, who grew stronger and better day by day. Pinocchio learned to make baskets and then sold them. With the money he received, he and his father were able to keep from starving.

In the evening the puppet studied hard. He succeeded not only in his studies but also in his work, and a day came when he put enough money together to keep his old father comfortable and happy. Besides this, he was able to save enough pennies to go to the marketplace and buy himself a new suit.

On the road on his way to buy this suit, he heard his name called.

He noticed a large Snail, who said to him, "Do you remember the Fairy with the Azure Hair?"

"Yes! What is she doing? Has she forgiven me? Does she remember me? Does she still love me? May I see her?"

"My dear Pinocchio, the Fairy is lying ill in a hospital. She has been stricken with trouble and illness, and she hasn't a penny left."

"Really? Oh, how sorry I am! My poor, dear little Fairy! If I had a million I should run to her with them!

But I have only fifty pennies. Here they are. I was just going to buy some new clothes. Here, take them, Snail, and give them to my good Fairy."

"What about the new clothes?"

"What does that matter? Come back here within a couple of days and I hope to have more money for you! Until today I have worked for my father. Now I shall have to work for my mother also."

The Snail, much against her usual habit, began to run like a lizard.

That night, Pinocchio, instead of going to bed at ten o'clock, waited until midnight, and instead of making eight baskets, he made sixteen.

After that he went to bed and fell asleep. As he slept, he dreamed of the Fairy, beautiful, smiling and happy, who kissed him and said to him, "Bravo, Pinocchio! In reward for your kind heart, I forgive you for all your old mischief. Boys who love and take good care of their parents when they are old and sick, deserve praise even though they may not be held up as models of obedience and good behavior. Keep on doing so well, and you will be happy."

At that very moment, Pinocchio awoke and opened his eyes wide.

What was his surprise and joy when, on looking himself over, he saw that he was no longer a puppet, but that he had become a real live boy! He looked all about him and instead of the usual walls of straw, he found himself in a beautifully furnished little room, the prettiest he had ever seen. In a twinkling, he jumped down from his bed to look at the chair standing near. There, he found a new suit, a new hat and a pair of shoes that fitted him perfectly.

As soon as he was dressed, he put his hands in his pockets and pulled out a little leather purse on which were written the following words:

"The Fairy with the Azure Hair returns fifty pennies to her dear Pinocchio with many thanks for his kind heart."

He opened the purse to find the money, and behold—there were fifty gold coins!

Pinocchio ran to the mirror. He hardly recognized himself. The bright face of a tall boy looked at him with wide-awake eyes, dark brown hair and happy, smiling lips.

"And where is Father?" he cried. He ran into the next room, and there stood Geppetto, grown years younger overnight, in new clothes. He was once more Mastro Geppetto, the wood-carver, hard at work on a lovely picture frame.

"Father, Father, what has happened?" cried Pinocchio, as he ran and jumped on his father's neck.

"This sudden change in our house is all your doing, my dear Pinocchio," answered Geppetto.

"What have I to do with it?"

"When bad boys become good and kind, they have the power of making their homes bright and new with happiness."

"I wonder where the old Pinocchio of wood has hidden himself?"

"There he is," said Geppetto. And he pointed to a large puppet leaning against a chair, head turned to one side, arms hanging limp and legs twisted under him.

After a long look, Pinocchio said to himself, "How ridiculous I was as a puppet! And now how happy I am, now that I have become a real boy!"

THE END